Trevor

Jim Averbeck

Pictures by Amy Hevron

A NEAL PORTER BOOK
ROARING BROOK PRESS
NEW YORK

To Dean, Patrice, Claudette, Leslie, and
ALL the friends who helped me come out of my cage —J.A.

For Honey, my first shy friend —A.H.

Text copyright © 2018 by Jim Averbeck

Illustrations copyright © 2018 by Amy Hevron

A Neal Porter Book

Published by Roaring Brook Press

Roaring Brook Press is a division of Holtzbrinck Publishing Holdings Limited Partnership

175 Fifth Avenue, New York, NY 10010

The art for this book was created using acrylic paint on wood and collaged digitally.

mackids.com

Library of Congress Control Number: 2017957305

ISBN: 978-1-250-14828-5

Our books may be purchased in bulk for promotional, educational, or business use. Please
contact your local bookseller or the Macmillan Corporate and Premium Sales Department
at (800) 221-7945 ext.5442 or by e-mail at MacmillanSpecialMarkets@macmillan.com

First edition 2018

Printed in China by Toppan Leefung Printing Ltd., Dongguan City, Guangdong Province

1 3 5 7 9 10 8 6 4 2

Trevor stretched his wings the width of his safe, boring cage.

Just a tiny peck and the door would pop open, but Trevor stayed—for the seeds.

He coveted the stripy ones. He
saved them for the loneliest days.
Today he was tempted to eat the
one he had hidden.

But then it would be gone.

So, though he had
no one to sing with, he
filled his lonesome
cage with song.

Churweeeeee

Outside, a tree stretched toward the sun, until a branch inched past the window frame, a lemon dangling from the end.

"Hello," said Trevor. "What a fine, plump canary you are. Will you sing with me?"

Chur

weeee
chiddle
chiddle

The lemon
said nothing.

"Oh," said Trevor, "you're shy. Maybe if I do something nice, you will sing with me."
Peck. POP.
Trevor pinched his treasured seed in his beak and flew out the window.

He deposited the seed on the branch.

"I've brought you a present," he told the lemon.

The lemon remained silent.

"I like presents, too," said Trevor, expectantly. But the lemon offered nothing.

Trevor hopped up and down, chittering and chattering. "My turn!" he cried. In all the commotion the seed fell and was lost in the dirt.

"Now see what you've done!" Trevor said.
"I'm not speaking to you."

He turned his back on the lemon . . .

and saw the vast, frightening world
stretched out before him.
He felt very lonely.

Trevor looked over his wing at the lemon.
"If you are sorry," said Trevor, "then don't
say a thing."

The lemon didn't.
"You're forgiven," said Trevor.

Trevor built a soft nest for himself and his friend.
The two huddled together through summer rains
and enjoyed warm sunny days. So did the striped seed,
which sprouted and grew.

Each morning, Trevor and
the lemon performed a duet.
Trevor sang the notes.

chur

weeeeee
chiddle chiddle

The lemon sang
the silences.

Trevor snuggled up to the lemon.
The lemon leaned back into Trevor.
"This is nice," said Trevor, "I am never,
ever leaving this nest."
   The lemon offered no opinion
on the wisdom of this.

That afternoon, a great dark cloud came over the horizon. The wind howled. Trevor pressed closer to his friend. A strong gust made their branch tremble. It was all Trevor could do to hang on.

With a *whoosh* and a *thump*, the lemon flew from the nest. It struck the sunflower below, scattering its seeds, then rolled out of sight.

Trevor leaped into the storm.
"Come back!" he called.

But when the storm cleared, his friend was gone.
Trevor cowered among the scattered seeds and wept.

"Are these seeds yours?" a voice asked.
"May we share them?" asked another.
Trevor wiped away his tears. Bright-eyed
birds fluttered around him. "Of course,"
he said. His friend would have wanted
it that way.

Before winter, Trevor and his new friends flew
to warmer climes, singing together along the way.

chirrup chee

chip chip

jee

cheer cheer

see it see it

chiddle chiddle chee

But he never forgot his first shy friend . . .

who gave him everything,
and asked for nothing at all.